Farmer Goff and His Turkey Sam

by Brian Schatell

E

J.B. Lippincott   New York

For Jeff

I would also like to thank
Mark, Lisa, and Betsy
without whom this book would not be

Farmer Goff and His Turkey Sam
Copyright © 1982 by Brian Schatell
All rights reserved. Printed in the United States of America.

Library of Congress Cataloging in Publication Data
Schatell, Brian.
   Farmer Goff and his turkey Sam.
   Summary: Sam the turkey would rather eat Mrs.
Goff's apple and turnip pies than win a blue ribbon
in the turkey contest at the county fair.
   [1. Turkeys—Fiction. 2. Fairs—Fiction]
I. Title.
PZ7.S336Far   1982   [E]   81-47756
ISBN 0-397-31982-7   AACR2
ISBN 0-397-31983-5 (lib. bdg.)

2 3 4 5 6 7 8 9 10

Farmer Goff lived on a small farm with his wife and a turkey named Sam.

Sam had won many blue ribbons for Farmer Goff in the turkey contests at the county fair. In fact, Sam had won so many blue ribbons, his owner was famous for miles around.

But there was nothing Farmer Goff loved to eat better than a roast turkey. He would often tell Sam with a snicker, "Good thing you win so many blue ribbons for me. If you didn't, I'd cook you for Thanksgiving dinner."

Sam, on the other hand, liked to eat Mrs. Goff's famous apple and turnip pies, which Farmer Goff always sold at the county fair. Every time Mrs. Goff put a pie out to cool, Sam would try to gobble it up.

Farmer Goff always warned Sam, "You're supposed to eat turkey feed! Stay away from pies, or else!"

The day before the county fair, Mrs. Goff baked lots and lots of pies. All day long, while he practiced his tricks for the fair, Sam heard loud baking noises and smelled delicious pielike smells coming from the kitchen, and he wished he could eat some pies.

The next morning, Sam saw Farmer Goff's truck piled high with pies on top of pies. He counted 294 apple and turnip pies in all!

Farmer Goff drove Sam and the pies to the fair.

When they got to the fairgrounds, Farmer Goff and Sam left the pies in the truck and took a place in the long line of turkeys and their owners.

Farmer Goff bragged loudly to the farmers next to him, "My turkey is going to win the blue ribbon in this contest, and it's all because *I* train him, and *I* feed him his turkey feed!"

This made Sam very mad. "Who wants turkey feed?" he thought angrily. "What good is winning blue ribbons if you can't eat pie??"

The contest began. The judge called out the first event: "Turkeys roll over!" and every turkey promptly rolled over — except Sam, who played dead. Then the judge called out, "Turkeys play dead!" and every turkey played dead — except for Sam, who rolled over.

The other farmers laughed at Farmer Goff.

Farmer Goff had never felt so embarrassed in his life!

He turned all sorts of colors,
like autumn leaves...

and jumped up and down
and tore at his hair...

and his ears steamed like
hot apple and turnip pie.

When the contest was over, Sam got the lowest score of any turkey. Farmer Goff was the laughing stock of the county fair.

"That does it," he screamed at Sam. "I'm going to eat you for Thanksgiving dinner!"

Sam didn't like that idea, and ran off into the fairgrounds. Farmer Goff grabbed his pitchfork and ran after him. But Sam was too fast, and he quickly disappeared into the crowd.

Farmer Goff looked everywhere…

but Sam was nowhere in sight.

After several hours, he started back toward his truck.
"Well, at least I can still sell those pies," he thought.

But when he got to his truck, the pies were gone!

"The pies! That blasted turkey ate all my pies!" he screamed.

Then he noticed a trail of crumbs that led from the truck
to a big tent nearby.

Farmer Goff ran inside, and sure enough, there was Sam
— and 294 empty apple and turnip pie tins — sitting at a
long table. Farmer Goff leaped toward Sam, his pitchfork
raised in the air.

"Fine turkey of yours," said a man to Farmer Goff. "He just won a blue ribbon in the pie-eating contest!"

Farmer Goff froze in midair as the contest judge presented him with a fancy blue ribbon.

"I'd hold on to that turkey for a while," the judge said admiringly. "How did you train him?"

"What?" said Farmer Goff in shock.

"He *what*?" Then slowly, he began to smile. "Oh! Well, I made him eat pies *every* day," he explained.

And then he posed for some pictures with Sam.

Afterward, Farmer Goff attached the ribbon to his windshield and drove Sam and the empty pie tins home.

"Well, Sam," he said, "it looks like you're going to win me a few more blue ribbons yet!"

Sam didn't feel so well after eating all those pies. He looked at the blue pie-eating ribbon, and he looked at Farmer Goff, and decided that at the next county fair, he just might go on a diet!

E
Schatell
Farmer Goff and his turkey Sam